DANGER RANGERS®

COOL BY THE POOL

Written by Ian Hopps
Edited by Jerry Houser
Art Direction by Susan J. Sullivan
Illustrated by Louis Scarborough and Ron LaChan

Revised and designed by Rocky Hill Group, Inc. and Judy O P...

D1401841

DANGER RANGERS®

Educational Adventures, LLC is proud to say that this book has
been approved as an excellent read-aloud storybook for young children by
a leading national literacy and reading expert. Professor Linda B. Gambrell of
the Eugene T. Moore School of Education at Clemson University is an author
and expert in the field of reading. Among Professor Gambrell's many distinctions, she is the
past president of the National Reading Conference, College Reading Association and was most
recently elected as president of the International Reading Association.

Produced in Association with
Safe Kids
WORLDWIDE®

This Danger Rangers book was produced in association with Safe Kids Worldwide, a global net-
work of organizations whose mission is to prevent accidental childhood injury, a leading killer of
children 14 and under. More than 450 coalitions in 16 countries bring together health and safety experts, educators, corporations, foundations, governments and volunteers to educate and protect families.   For more information on how to protect your child, please visit www.safekids.org.

The Danger Rangers is the exclusive property of

entertain · educate · empower
E3A
educational
adventures
www.e3a.com

DANGER RANGERS ®

Dear Parents,

Splash! Splash! On a hot day, children find frolicking in water at the pool, lake or beach refreshing. Experiencing their bodies immersed in the wonders of water is uniquely delightful.

Learning to feel comfortable in the water is a time of celebration for most children. And mastering the physical challenges necessary to swim fosters a well-deserved sense of accomplishment.

Exposure to water play brings a wealth of benefits for children. Parents should make an effort to engage such opportunities; they can be splendid family outings. Some caregivers fear water because of the oft-recited – and real – dangers. But if parents and caregivers always actively supervise children around water and the entire family is knowledgeable about basic water safety rules, the risks are greatly reduced.

Cool by the Pool includes these important rules. In this adventurous tale, children are having a pool party where risky behaviors run amok. In the nick of time, the Danger Rangers come down to prevent potentially serious injuries. Excitement heightens as they capture the villain responsible for hazards designed to spoil the fun for the hearty partygoers.

Kids and parents will learn a lot from this story about water safety rules. The mighty Danger Rangers show, once again, that children can be safe and have a lot of fun, too.

—Alvin F. Poussaint, M.D.

Dr. Poussaint is Professor of Psychiatry at Harvard Medical School and the Judge Baker Children's Center in Boston.

Born and raised in East Harlem in a family of eight children, Dr. Poussaint graduated from Columbia University and received his M.D. from Cornell University. He then took postgraduate training at UCLA Neuropsychiatric Institute, where he served as Chief Resident in Psychiatry.

Dr. Poussaint served as a script consultant to NBC's The Cosby Show *and continues to consult to the media as an advocate of more responsible programming. He is a regular consultant for children's books, television shows and movies.*

Squeeky

Burt

Sully

Burble

Gabriela

Kitty

Meet the

DANGER RANGERS®

These six brave superheroes of safety are out to make the world a safer place by eliminating one danger at a time. From their secret headquarters, the Danger Rangers are ready to leap into action at a moment's notice!

SULLY is the leader and spokes-seal. He's safety-driven, smart, and funny.

KITTY is cool, smart and adventurous. She's the brains of the team.

BURBLE is the team's heart and soul, the power-house and practical joker.

BURT is the very creative and part-genius Personal Safety expert.

GABRIELA is the highly skilled Chief of Operations and head safety trainer.

SQUEEKY may be the smallest Danger Ranger, but he's also the loudest. Good things come in small packages.

CHAPTER I
Pool Party

Annie Barker was having a pool party. Inside the closed gates around the pool area, there were kids swimming, splashing and jumping into the pool everywhere you looked. Annie was in the shallow end of the pool with her friend George Whiskers.

"Are you wishing for something special for your birthday?" asked George.

"I wish I could be a Junior Danger Ranger just like you," said Annie.

"That'd be great!" said George. "But you don't get that as a present. You have to earn it. You always have to be alert and on the lookout for possible dangers around you."

"I think I could do that," said Annie.

SAVO says: Swimmers should stay out of the diving area when someone is diving.

"OK," said George, pointing toward the deep end of the pool. "Tell me what you see over there."

Annie looked and saw her friend Julie about to jump into the pool. She also saw her little brother Joey swimming across the pool, right in front of the diving board.

"Julie! Don't jump!" she yelled.

Always swim in the designated swimming areas.

Annie and George ran over and lifted Joey out of the pool.

"That was a close call," said Annie. "She could have landed on your head."

"Always remember to swim in the designated swimming area or in the shallow end," said George.

"Right!" said Annie. "And never swim under or near the diving board when someone is ready to jump off."

9

George turned and looked around the backyard. "Is there a lifeguard here?" he asked.

"Yeah," said Annie. "My dad is our lifeguard."

"Looks like your dad could use some help," said George. "I'm giving the Danger Rangers a call."

CHAPTER 2

Cooling Down

On a hot day, drink plenty of liquids to keep cool.

ALERT

"Come on Rangers! Pick up the pace," ordered SAVO, as Sully, Kitty and the gang continued their exercises.

Suddenly, Burble set down his dumbbells and headed inside.

Burble returned with a tray of lemonade!

"Good move Burble," said Squeeky. "You always have to drink plenty of liquids when you're exercising, especially on a hot day like today."

"Right! When it's this hot, you could get dehydrated from sweating too much," said Kitty.

"Or you could get too hot and get sick," added Burt.

"**BE SMART**. Don't overdo it on a hot day," said Kitty.

"Calling all Danger Rangers!" blared SAVO over the loudspeakers. "We have a danger alert from one of our Junior Danger Rangers. Pool party perils abound!"

"Let's go!" shouted Kitty. "Everyone to the launch bay!"

Sully, Squeeky, Burble, and Burt fell in line behind her and together they yelled, "**SAFETY RULES!**"

CHAPTER 3

Fun in the Sun

Kitty landed the hovercraft across the street. Annie introduced herself and led them all to her backyard.

George hurried over to say hello. "Thanks for coming, Danger Rangers," he said. "I noticed a few dangers and I didn't want anyone to get hurt."

"We wouldn't want that to happen either," agreed Kitty.

15

Annie led the Danger Rangers around the pool so they could meet her dad.

"I like your clown," said Sully. He pointed to the birthday clown nearby who walked with a waddle and laughed with a funny snort.

For a moment, Kitty thought she saw several small, shadowy figures peek out from behind the clown's big coat. She blinked and looked again. There was no one there. The clown just smiled.

"Danger Rangers, this is my dad," said Annie. "He's our lifeguard for the day."

"Hi, Mr. Barker," said Burt. "We're here to help you with the kids."

"And clear up any dangers," Sully added.

"Thanks," said Mr. Barker, looking relieved. "I can sure use the help. There are lots of parents here watching, but I need someone whose only job is to watch the kids in the water."

Just then, a boy ran past them and slipped in a puddle.

"Whoooaa!" the boy yelled as he fell back.

"Gotcha!" Burble shouted. "Be careful there little fellow. It's usually slippery around a pool, so don't run. It's never a safe thing to do."

"OK, let's spread out," said Sully. "We've got a little party patrolling to do. And be careful not to trip on those inner tubes and rafts that are lying around the pool."

Never run near a pool—you could slip and fall.

18

Always wear sunscreen when you're out in the sun.

"Good idea," said Burt. "Oh, don't forget the sunscreen. We don't want to get burned on duty."

Annie reached for her bottle of sunscreen but it wasn't there. "Hey, my sunscreen is gone!"

"Not a problem," said Squeeky. "A Danger Ranger always comes prepared."

As Squeeky handed his sunscreen to Annie, a tiny shadowy figure with a big bottle of sunscreen ran behind the clown. The clown smiled and gave a little laugh with a funny snort.

CHAPTER 4
A Secret Thief

Squeeky rolled a big inner tube to a safe place at the side of the pool. When he stopped to catch his breath, Squeeky thought he saw something run behind the clown. He walked over to him. "Excuse me. Did you happen to see a little guy run past here?" he asked.

The clown just stared at him and gave a little laugh with a funny snort.

Squeeky looked around, but there was nothing there. "Must be the heat," he thought to himself.

Meanwhile, Sully and Burble were giving diving lessons.

"Now, remember, before you ever dive into a pool, make sure diving is allowed," said Sully. "You should ask the owner, the lifeguard or the adult in charge if it's OK."

"And only dive in the deep end of the pool," said Burble. He tapped his head with his finger. "**USE YOUR HEAD**. Don't hit your head!"

Only dive in the deep end and only if diving is allowed.

"Also, make sure the coast is clear before you dive," added Sully.

"That's right!" said Squeeky. He climbed up on the diving board and checked to make sure no one was in the diving area. "All clear!" he shouted.

"Remember," said Squeeky, "only jump on the diving board when you've been taught how to do it." With that he did a perfect double-flip twister dive, but when he looked down at the pool, the water had vanished! It was gone!

Look before you leap—especially when you dive.

Leaping into action, Burble reached out just in time and caught Squeeky in mid-air.

Kitty looked over the side. "Wow! The pool is empty!" she said.

"No one should ever play around an empty pool," reminded Sully.

"My party is ruined!" cried Annie. She started to cry. "Even the clown is gone!"

Everyone looked around. It was true. The strange clown who walked with a waddle and laughed with a funny snort was gone.

"Wait! I have an idea!" said Kitty. She put her arm around Annie. "Why don't we all go down to the lake?"

"That's a great idea!" said Sully. "There's lots of water there."

All the parents agreed. Everyone quickly packed up their stuff and before you could say, "Happy birthday, Annie!" the party was on its way to the lake.

CHAPTER 5

Lakeside Fun

"This is going to be so much fun," exclaimed Annie, as they arrived at the lake.

"I found the perfect spot," said Burble. "It's close enough to the water so the parents can keep an eye on all of the kids."

"And it's close to the ice cream," said Sully licking his lips.

The ice cream man was wearing a big hat that covered his face. When he walked, he had a familiar waddle and gave a little laugh with a funny snort.

George grabbed a ball. "Let's play catch." He kicked his sandals off.

"George, wait!" shouted Annie. "You should never go barefoot. You don't know what might be buried in the sand."

"Good point," said Burt. "Wearing sandals is always the smart way to go."

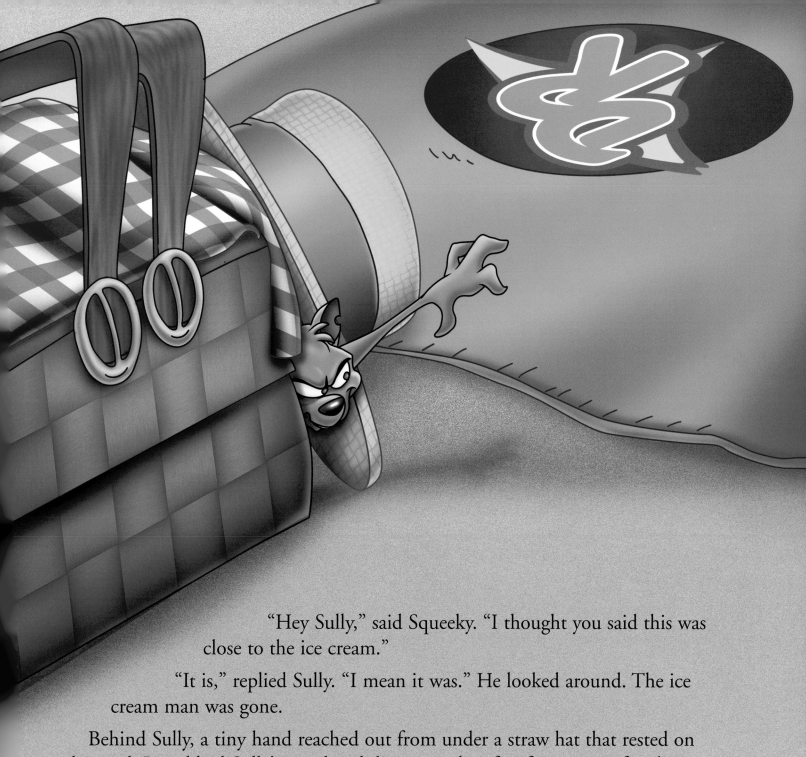

"Hey Sully," said Squeeky. "I thought you said this was close to the ice cream."

"It is," replied Sully. "I mean it was." He looked around. The ice cream man was gone.

Behind Sully, a tiny hand reached out from under a straw hat that rested on the sand. It grabbed Sully's towel and disappeared. A few feet away, a familiar-looking figure peeked out from behind a tree, picked up the big sun hat, and waddled off, giving a little laugh and a funny snort.

27

CHAPTER 6

More Fun in the Sun

Never swim unless a lifeguard or adult is watching.

All the kids gathered around Sully at the edge of the lake. "OK, everyone!" yelled Sully. "Annie's father is going to be your lifeguard."

"Make sure he can see you at all times," added Kitty.

"And make sure you **BUDDY-UP**," said Burt. "You should never go swimming alone. You should always swim with another person."

Never swim alone.
Always buddy-up.

Nearby, Burt paddled along in the water. Squeeky sat on top of his shell keeping watch. A little boy was swimming along by himself. Burt quickly swam over to him.

"How come you don't have a water buddy?" asked Burt.

"I don't need one," answered the boy. "I'm a good swimmer."

"Whoa!" said Burt. "It doesn't matter how good a swimmer you are, you should never swim alone."

Squeeky splashed into the water. "I'll be your water buddy!" he said.

29

Back on shore, the ice cream man stood by the drinking fountain. He leaned over and twisted the handle. Water squirted out, but the ice cream man didn't take a drink. Instead, he bent down and connected something to the back of the fountain.

A few minutes later, Burble twisted the handle on the drinking fountain but nothing came out! "Hey! Where did all the water go?" he asked.

Then Joey bent down and opened up the party picnic basket, but it was empty, too.

"I'm checking this out!" said Squeeky.

Squeeky walked all around the drinking fountain trying to find some clues. No luck. All he found were some ice cream sticks and crumpled-up wrappers. Then he tripped over something. It was a bamboo pipe! He looked closely at the pipe. It led from the drinking fountain into some nearby trees.

"This pipe must be draining all the water from the drinking fountain!" said Squeeky.

Together, the Danger Rangers followed the bamboo pipe into the trees. Along the way, they found more things dropped on the ground. There was a bottle of sunscreen, a beach towel and a popped balloon.

Finally, they came to a wooden gate.

"This must be where all the water is going," said Kitty.

Burt looked up and read from a broken-down old sign, "Wally's Water Park. Enter at your own risk!"

33

CHAPTER 7

Enter at Your Own Risk

The Danger Rangers saw several rickety water slides made from pieces of rusted metal and rotten wood. Crooked, broken ladders led up to wobbly slides.

"What kind of water park is this?" asked Sully.

"Not a very safe one, that's for sure," said Burt. "No wonder the sign said enter at your own risk!"

Kitty stared at a rusty slide. "Who would use a place like this?" she wondered.

Suddenly, they heard a familiar laugh and voice come from behind them. "I would," it said with a funny snort. "Allow me to introduce myself. I'm Wally."

"You look just like the clown at the party and the ice cream man from the lake!" said Squeeky.

"That's because . . . I am!" declared Wally.

"Did you steal the water from the drinking fountain at the lake and Annie's pool?" asked Sully.

"That was me!" Wally said proudly. "With a little help from Tip, Pip & Company – my partners in crime."

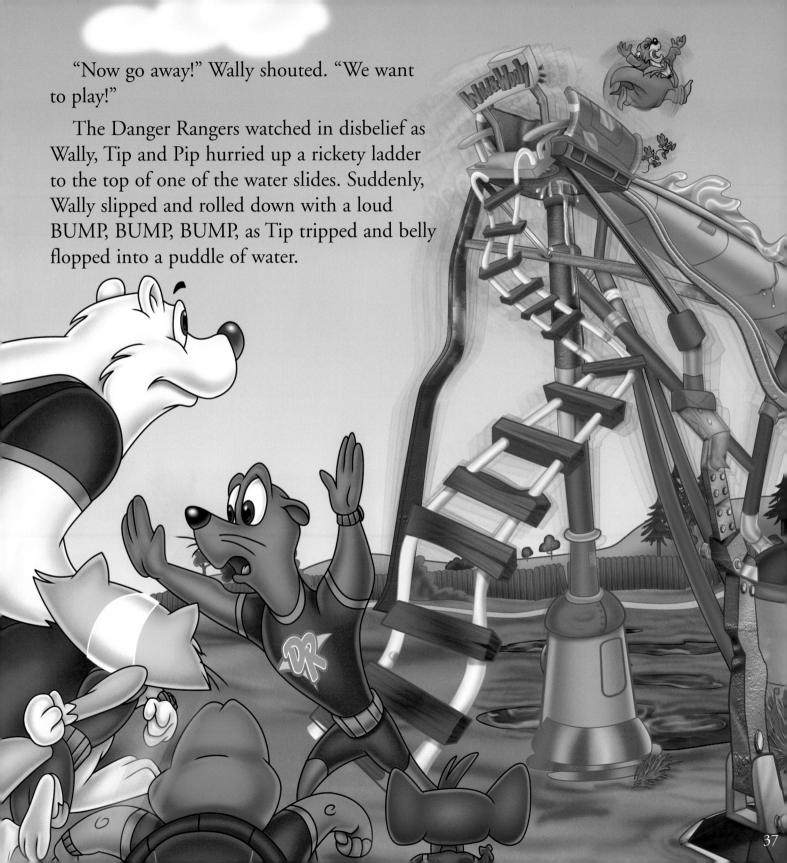

"Now go away!" Wally shouted. "We want to play!"

The Danger Rangers watched in disbelief as Wally, Tip and Pip hurried up a rickety ladder to the top of one of the water slides. Suddenly, Wally slipped and rolled down with a loud BUMP, BUMP, BUMP, as Tip tripped and belly flopped into a puddle of water.

"Come down from that slide before you really get hurt!" yelled Sully.

Suddenly, the towering water slide started to shake and twist. It swayed back and forth and side to side. The water slide CREAKED! It CRAAAACKED and collapsed!

Wally, Tip and Pip were tossed high into the air.

39

"I got 'em!" yelled Burt. He pulled out his Porto-Pool and yanked on the cord. WHOOSH! It inflated and filled with water.

SPLASH, SPLASH, SPLASH! Wally, Tip and Pip landed safely in the Porto-Pool.

CHAPTER 8
Crime Never Pays

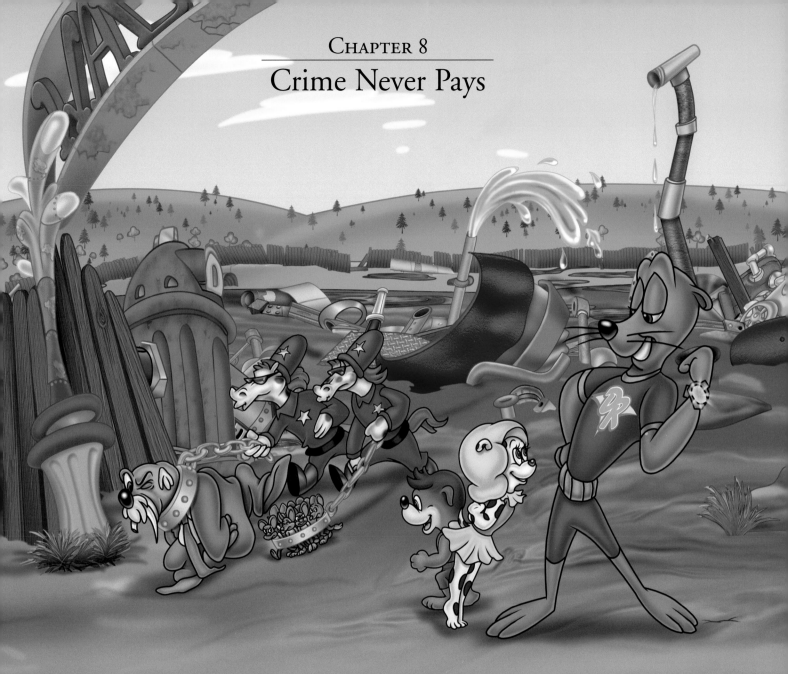

Outside the broken-down water park, Wally and his gang were led away by the police.

"I'm glad no one got hurt," said Kitty.

"Good move calling the police, Annie," said Sully.

Annie smiled. "It was easy," she said. "Whenever there's trouble or an emergency, you always call the police or 911."

Kitty smiled. She was very proud of Annie.

"Hey, hey, hey. What about the party?" asked Burt.

"You go ahead," said Squeeky. "Sully and I are going to return the water where it belongs." Sully grabbed onto the wheel of a big water valve and started to turn it.

"Well, what are we waiting for?" shouted Kitty. "There's a party at Annie's house!"

CHAPTER 9
Birthday Surprise!

"Now, how about opening those gifts?" asked Squeeky, as he handed Annie a box.

Inside was a Junior Danger Ranger badge that glistened like sunlight. Burt helped Annie pin on her badge.

"You're now an official Junior Danger Ranger in training," said Burt.

"Thanks!" said Annie. "I'll wear it all the time!"

Annie's mom came out of the house carrying the largest birthday cake Annie had ever seen. Everyone joined in and sang "Happy Birthday." Annie took a deep breath and blew out all of the candles.

"Cake time!" shouted Squeeky.

CHAPTER 10

Rules of the Pool

The next day, all the Danger Rangers gathered together in the debriefing room inside their secret headquarters.

"Good job team!" said SAVO. "You really made a big splash at the party!"

"Yeah! And it's nice to know those kids learned all those important water safety rules," said Sully. "Now, they'll know how to have fun in the sun and stay safe!"

"OK, let's review," said Kitty. She pulled out her notebook and flipped it open.

Rules of the Pool

1. Never swim if there isn't a lifeguard or an adult watching.
2. Always swim in the designated swimming areas.
3. Never swim alone. Always buddy-up with a water buddy.
4. Only dive in the deep end of the pool and only after you have made sure diving is allowed.
5. Look before you leap, especially when you're diving into a pool.
6. Swimmers should stay away from the diving area when someone is diving.
7. Never run near a pool – you could slip and fall.
8. On a hot day, be sure to drink plenty of liquids to keep your body cool.
9. Always wear sunscreen when you're out in the sun.
10. Be alert when barefoot. Better yet, wear beach shoes or sandals.

Kitty closed her notebook. "This case, Cool by the Pool, is officially closed!"